Magic
mal Friends

Special thanks to Valerie Wilding

ORCHARD BOOKS

First published in Great Britain in 2016 by The Watts Publishing Group

1 3 5 7 9 10 8 6 4 2

A CIP catalogue record for this book is available from the British Library.

ISBN 978 1 40834 123 0

Printed in Great Britain

The paper and board used in this book are made from wood from responsible sources

Orchard Books
An imprint of Hachette Children's Group
Part of The Watts Publishing Group Limited
Carmelite House, 50 Victoria Embankment, London EC4Y 0DZ

An Hachette UK Company
www.hachette.co.uk
www.hachettechildrens.co.uk

Holly Santapaws Saves Christmas

Daisy Meadows

Sunshine Meadow

Honey Tree

Goldie's Grotto

Toadstool Cafe

Toadstool Glade

Mrs Taptree's Library

Friendship Tree

Parasol Tree

Grizelda's Workshop

Spark

Fall

Rushing Rapids

Butterfly Bower

En

to th

Heart Trees

Nibblesqueak Bakery

Map of Friendship Forest
Woollyhop Shop
Harmony Hall Theatre
Petal Hill
Garland Green
Cherry Tree Corner
Treasure Tree
Bluebell Brook
Agatha, Glitterwing's Shop
Slipperslide's Home
Sparklepaw Cottage
Coral Cove
Summer Sands Beach
Witchy Waste
Grizelda's Tower

Can you keep a secret? I thought you could!

Then I'll tell you about an enchanted wood.

It lies through the door in the old oak tree,

Let's go there now - just follow me!

We'll find adventure that never ends,

And meet the Magic Animal Friends!

Love,

Goldie the Cat

Story One
Christmas Bells

CHAPTER ONE

Toasty Toffees

"Shoo!" Lily Hart chased two wild geese away from her mum's cabbage plants. Her best friend, Jess Forester, helped guide the greedy birds to the Harts' new pond.

Nearby was the Helping Paw Wildlife Hospital, which Lily's parents ran in a barn in their garden. The poorly animals

were inside, but those who were getting better were in pens outside enjoying fresh air. Winter sunlight shone through bare trees, making spiky shadows on the grass. Mrs Hart was putting out bowls of juicy lettuce and crunchy carrots for bunnies, guinea pigs and tortoises to enjoy.

"Offer the geese this," she said, handing the girls some spinach and lettuce.

"That will keep them off my veggies. It's turning colder, so they'll soon fly off to somewhere warmer."

"Will they go together?" asked Jess.

Mrs Hart nodded. "A pair of geese are partners for life," she said, as she wandered away to feed some baby badgers.

"Like being married!" Lily whispered.

The girls shared a smile as they watched the geese eagerly tucking into the leaves.

"We'll soon be going to a real wedding in Friendship Forest," Jess said excitedly.

Lily slipped a white card from her pocket. It was leaf-shaped, and decorated with frosted silver bells. It read,

"You are invited to
the winter wedding of
Mr Cleverfeather to Miss Sweetbeak
in Silver Glade, Friendship Forest
and to a celebration at the
Toadstool Café.

Lily laughed. "Whoever thought we'd see two owls get married!"

Friendship Forest was a secret magical world, where the animals lived in little cottages and dens. And they could all

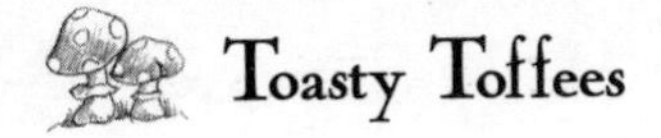

talk! The girls' friend Goldie the cat often came to take them to the forest, where they'd had amazing adventures. One morning, they had each found a wedding invitation tucked inside their welly boots. They knew that Goldie must have delivered them.

"I'm looking forward to meeting Miss Sweetbeak," Jess began, when something caught her eye. She looked closely at the reflections in the pond. Between

her and Lily was a third reflection. A cat!

"Goldie!" she cried and turned to see a cat with golden fur and eyes as green as Mrs Hart's lettuce.

Lily clutched Jess's hand in excitement. "Does this mean it's time for the wedding?"

Instantly, Goldie ran down the garden, across the stepping stones in Brightley Stream and into Brightley Meadow.

The girls raced after her as she headed for an old, dead-looking tree.

As Goldie drew near, the tree burst into life. Glossy, deep green leaves sprang

from its branches and red-breasted robins hopped from twig to twig, feasting on scarlet berries. Squirrels scampered up and down the trunk, gathering nuts for their winter store.

When Lily and Jess reached Goldie she touched a paw to the tree. They read aloud two words written in the bark.

"Friend … ship … For … est!"

A door appeared in the trunk. Jess turned its leaf-shaped handle and opened it.

The girls followed Goldie inside, stepping into golden light. Instantly, they felt the tingle that meant they were shrinking, just a little.

When the shimmering light faded, Jess and Lily found themselves among the trees of Friendship Forest. Big, soft snowflakes drifted around them.

"It's snowing!" Lily cried in delight. "That means the Winter Wonders are back!"

The magical Winter Wonders were a sugarplum, a snowflake and a silver-tipped snowdrop. They brought a beautiful glittering winter to Friendship Forest.

"Isn't it lovely?" said a soft voice.

The girls turned to see Goldie, standing upright, with her glittery scarf around her shoulders.

"Hello!" they cried, running to hug her.

"I hope we're here for the wedding," said Jess, "and not because horrid Grizelda's causing problems."

The witch Grizelda was desperate to drive the animals out of Friendship Forest, so she could have it for herself. So far, Goldie and the girls had managed to stop her wicked plans, but they knew she'd never give up.

"Grizelda hasn't been around, which is good news." Goldie grinned. "The other good news is that the wedding's tomorrow, but today someone's come to meet you!"

A tiny white puppy wearing a red hat trimmed with fluffy white swansdown bounced towards them. She pulled a little

red sledge decorated with tinkling silver bells.

"Meet Holly Santapaws!" said Goldie.

"Happy Christmas Eve, Jess and Lily!" cried Holly. Her dark eyes sparkled.

"Christmas Eve?" Lily asked, scooping her up for a hug.

Holly nodded.

"Of course!" said Jess, tickling the puppy's ears. "Time is different in Friendship Forest."

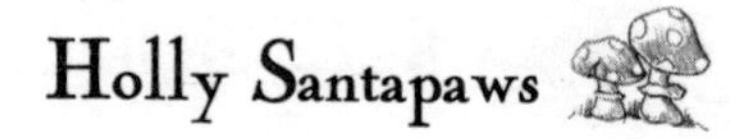

"If today is Christmas Eve, and tomorrow is Mr Cleverfeather's wedding ..." said Lily, "that means Mr Cleverfeather's getting married on Christmas Day!"

"Wow!" said Jess. "That's so exciting!"

"I'm going to the wedding too!" the puppy said. "I'm Mr Cleverfeather's apprentice. When I grow up, I'm going to be an inventor, just like him!" She jumped down and fetched a jar from her sledge.

"Have a sweet," she said, opening the jar. "They're Toasty Toffees. When you eat them, they keep you toasty warm. I

invented them!"

"Ooh, lovely," said Lily. "It's chilly today." She reached into the jar. "Oh!"

"What's wrong?" Holly asked.

"I think maybe the sweets are too warm," said Lily. "They've melted together!"

The puppy looked so sad about the sweets that Lily quickly added, "I bet they're delicious though."

"Another of my inventions has gone wrong," said Holly, her tail drooping.

Jess hugged her. "I bet you have other great inventions, though."

Goldie smiled. "I know what will cheer Holly up," she said. "Miss Sweetbeak wants the three of you to visit the boutique where she makes beautiful clothes."

Jess and Lily glanced at each other, thrilled.

"We're going to meet the bride!" said Lily. "But why does she want to see us?"

Goldie smiled. "Let's find out!"

CHAPTER TWO

Ice Creatures

Friendship Forest looked so different as the friends walked along. It sounded different too, with Christmas bells tinkling among the branches.

"It's so magical!" said Lily.

Decorated Christmas trees stood outside the tiny cottages. The Twinkletail mice had a teeny candle in every window of their home, which was perched on a tree branch. There were holly wreaths on all the front doors and as they passed Agatha Glitterwing the magpie's house, they heard her singing, "Deck the hall with seeds and berries, Tra-la-la-la-laa, la-la-la-laa."

They reached a red door in a large silver birch tree. Snowflake decorations were tied to every branch with silver lace bows and the windows were draped with sparkling white fabric that looked like snowdrifts. A sign said, “Miss Sweetbeak’s Unique Boutique.” Goldie knocked on the door.

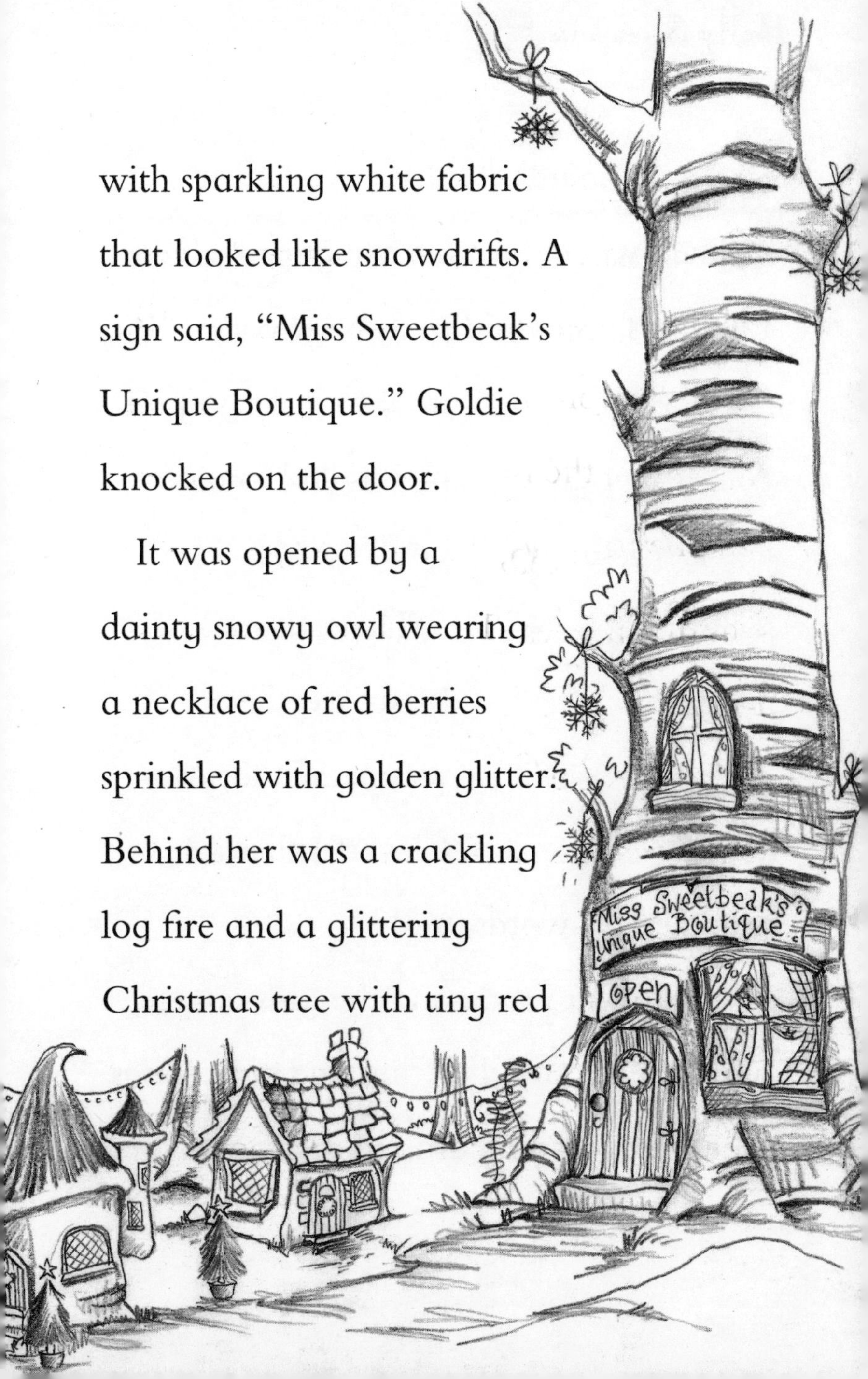

It was opened by a dainty snowy owl wearing a necklace of red berries sprinkled with golden glitter. Behind her was a crackling log fire and a glittering Christmas tree with tiny red and gold lights.

The owl clapped her wingtips. "Hello, my dears!" she said in a sweet voice. "I'm

mad to gleet you – I mean glad to meet you!"

The girls smiled. Miss Sweetbeak was perfect for Mr Cleverfeather. He muddled his words, too!

They went inside and the girls gasped at all the beautiful clothes and accessories that were hanging around the room.

They could see Miss Sweetbeak was very talented indeed! They all sat down on heaps of Christmassy cushions in red, green and silver.

"I made these," said Miss Sweetbeak, patting a silver cushion embroidered with gold writing.

The girls giggled. The letters said "Bingle jells!"

"Now, my dears," said the snowy owl. "It's cold, so I'll give you coats to keep you warm." She bustled to a rail and fetched a blue coat with a peacock feather collar for Lily and a purple one trimmed with creamy lambswool for Jess.

"Thanks!" they said.

"Mr Cleverfeather and I would like to thank you for everything you've done for our forest," said Miss Sweetbeak. "So … Jess and Lily, will you be my bridesmaids?"

The girls gasped.

"And Holly," said Miss Sweetbeak, "will you be my flower girl?"

Lily and Jess were thrilled. They threw their arms around the snowy owl and said, "We can't wait!"

Holly was bouncing in circles with

excitement!

Miss Sweetbeak fetched two pretty red dresses, trimmed with tiny white feathers.

Lily squealed. “Are they bridesmaid dresses?”

Miss Sweetbeak nodded.

Goldie stroked the fluffy white cuffs. “This is so soft.”

“Those downy feathers are from when

I was a baby," said Miss Sweetbeak. "I saved them for my wedding day."

Holly couldn't stop bouncing. "The dresses are perfect for a Christmas wedding," she said. "They match my hat!"

Miss Sweetbeak hopped up and down herself. "I always moped to get harried on Christmas Day!" She laughed. "I mean hoped to get married!"

"I love Christmas," said Holly. "I like to

give people my inventions as presents!"

Lily looked around the boutique. There were satin capes for squirrels, with huge pockets for nut-gathering, velvet bonnets with holes for bunnies' ears, and a rail of party dresses with matching headbands.

"You must be busy, Miss Sweetbeak," said Jess. "Can we help?"

"Yes, please," said the owl. "Could you take Mr Cleverfeather his wedding present while I bop the puttons – I mean, pop the buttons – on your dresses?" She gave Jess a parcel tied with silver ribbon. "It's a waistcoat that I embroidered especially for him."

"What a brilliant gift!" said Lily. "Of course we'll take it."

The four friends set off. When they reached Mr Cleverfeather's inventing shed, high in a tree, the girls were surprised to see a little round workshop nearby. It was dusted with snow, and shining icicles hung from the roof. A sign over the door said "Holly's Wonders Workshop."

"That's where I work," the puppy said proudly. "I'll show you later."

Goldie pressed her paw against Mr Cleverfeather's tree. The bark rippled and twisted, until a spiral staircase appeared.

Up they went, calling, "Hello!"

Mr Cleverfeather opened the door. "Goldie! And Less and Jilly," he said, muddling his words and flapping his wings anxiously. "Hittle Lolly, too!"

"Are you all right, Mr Cleverfeather?"

Jess asked the owl.

"We brought a gift from Miss Sweetbeak," added Holly.

Mr Cleverfeather opened the parcel. "What … a … lovely … present," he said slowly, then closed his eyes. "I feel even worse now!"

The girls shared a worried glance. "What's wrong?" Lily asked.

The owl took a deep breath. "I'm trying to finish my presents for Miss Sweetbeak, but everything's rowing gong! I mean going wrong. I've lost my Ice Device – my ice sculpting invention.

The Confetti Shower won't work. Nor will the Merry Melody Machine." He sighed. "The Sparklehoof reindeer haven't arrived with the wedding sleigh, either. I must find them and get my inventions working for my wedding day."

"The girls and I will find the Sparklehoofs," Goldie said gently.

"I'll fix the Confetti Shower in my

workshop," said Holly, "while you work on the Merry Melody Machine."

"Thank you mo such," said Mr Cleverfeather. "I mean …"

But the four friends were already going downstairs. Jess and Lily carried the Confetti Shower between them. It was a box covered with multi-coloured polka dots, and something that looked like a hose attached to the front, which flopped all over the place.

The girls put the Confetti Shower down outside Holly's workshop and went in. A little stove burned in the corner,

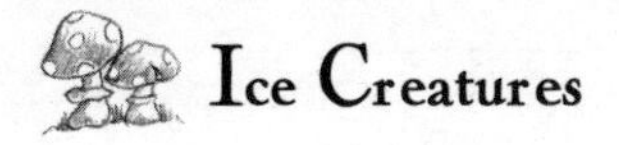

making it warm and cosy. White baskets were lined up on a shelf. Labels showed that they were filled with useful things, like cardboard tubes, sticky tape, wool and buttons.

On another shelf were inventions Holly was working on, and on the top shelf was

a row of Toasty Toffee jars.

Lily saw a pair of shiny shoes on a bench. "Did you make those?" she asked Holly.

"Yes." The puppy looked downcast. "Mr Cleverfeather thinks he can't dance, so I invented special dancing shoes for him to make sure he could on his wedding day. But the trouble is—"

"Look!" cried Goldie, pointing through the open doorway. "What's that shadow?"

CHAPTER THREE

Filth in the Forest

A sleigh, drawn by three animals, was flying through the air towards them! Jess, Lily, Goldie and Holly ran outside to get a closer look.

"Is it the Sparklehoofs, coming for the wedding?" asked Jess.

"I'm not sure," Goldie said.

As the sleigh drew nearer, they saw it was made of ice. The creatures pulling it were made of ice, too, with icicles sticking up from their heads, like horns. Even their coats were made of jagged chunks of ice instead of fur.

"What are they?" Holly cried, her voice shaking a little.

The sleigh flew lower, landed and slid to a stop in the snow. The horrified girls

recognised the driver.

"Grizelda!" Jess gasped.

"What does she want?" Lily cried.

Grizelda's green hair whipped around her bony face, and her cloak swirled over her purple tunic and skinny black trousers. She stamped her pointy-toed boot, cried, "Yaaah!" and urged her ice creatures forward.

"Look out!" Jess yelled. "She's heading straight for us!"

Lily swept Holly into her arms. The girls dived one way and Goldie the other, to avoid the charging ice creatures.

Grizelda yanked on the reins to halt the sleigh. She jumped out and snatched up the Confetti Shower.

"Ha!" she cackled. "I've got your stupid machine!"

Jess wanted to snatch it back, but Grizelda's ice creatures stamped and pawed the snowy ground. She didn't dare go near those icy hooves.

Grizelda pointed at the machine. Sparks flew from her finger.

"She's casting a spell!" Lily cried.

Holly buried her face in her paws as Grizelda chanted:

"Take this stupid Confetti Flinger,

Transform it to a dirty slinger.

Filthy blaster, I'm your master

Make the forest a disaster!"

Grizelda aimed the machine's nozzle at a tree. Instead of confetti, it spat muck. In seconds, the tree was covered in dirt.

"Stop!" Lily yelled.

"Ha! I'll cover the forest with muck," the witch shrieked. "Christmas will be ruined! And when the snow melts,

there'll be filth all over the animals' homes. They'll all have to leave, and then the forest will be mine!"

She climbed back into the sleigh and shook the reins, and the ice creatures pulled the sleigh into the air. Grizelda fired dirt from the Confetti Shower at everything she passed.

Jess was shocked. "She'll ruin Christmas, and she'll ruin the wedding, too!"

Holly's eyes filled with tears. "Poor Mr Cleverfeather," she whispered. "Poor Miss Sweetbeak."

Lily hugged her and said, "Jess, we must stop Grizelda before she ruins Christmas, the wedding – and the entire forest!"

"But how?" Goldie said miserably.

"Is there anything you have invented recently, that we could use?" Jess asked.

The little puppy said sadly, "There were the dancing shoes for Mr Cleverfeather, but they went wrong. They won't stop dancing." Her ears drooped. "I'm not a very good inventor."

Lily scooped Holly up and cuddled her. "You are!" she said.

But Holly said tearfully, "Everything's gone wrong. Even my Toasty Toffees."

Lily's face lit up. "Toasty Toffees! Maybe they're sticky enough to plug up the Confetti Shower and stop the dirt!"

"That's brilliant!" said Jess.

The puppy's ears perked up. "Do you think it would work?"

"Let's try!" said Lily.

Back in Holly's Wonders Workshop, Goldie filled a basket with Toasty Toffees. Then they set off in search of Grizelda.

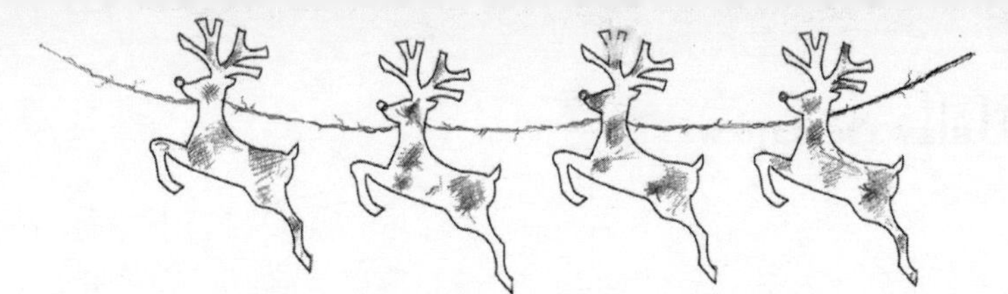

The witch had already made a hideous mess of the forest. Even the tree decorations were mucky, and the Christmas bells couldn't ring because they were full of dirt.

Jess ran her hand over a chain of cut-out paper reindeer. Her fingers came away filthy. "Ugh!" she said. "The dirt's so greasy it sticks to everything."

They hurried on, but when they reached Miss Sweetbeak's Unique Boutique, they stared in horror.

It was covered in greasy mud, just like everything else in the forest.

Lily flung open the door and cried out. "Oh no!"

The girls' bridesmaids' dresses were filthy. And Miss Sweetbeak's wedding dress was splattered with muck.

With a sad hoot, the snowy owl's face appeared from behind the shop counter.

"Everything is ruined," she cried.

Holly gave a yip. "Wait here, everyone!" She scurried off, her white paws growing dirtier as she ran through the muck.

"Holly!" Jess cried in alarm. "Where are you going?"

CHAPTER FOUR

Bubble Power

Goldie cleaned the kettle and made blackberry tea for Miss Sweetbeak.

Jess watched out for Holly, while Lily smoothed the owl's white feathers. "There, there," she said. "It'll be all right."

"Thank you, my dears," Miss Sweetbeak said shakily. "But I don't hoe

now – I mean, know how."

"Holly's coming!" Jess called.

The little puppy burst into the boutique, clutching a bottle of crystals labelled "Bubble Flower Paint Power."

"I made it from the bubble flowers that grow by the river," she panted. "It was supposed to turn things blue. But it went wrong. It didn't paint things, it cleaned them. I'll have to change the label."

Jess peered at the tiny blue-green crystals. "How does it work?" she asked.

"You mix it with water," Holly explained, "then it bubbles all over the dirt

and cleans anything you want to clean." She smiled at Miss Sweetbeak. "Even the special dresses for the wedding, and all the lovely clothes you've made."

The snowy owl threw her wings around Holly. "Thank you!"

Lily dropped a kiss on the puppy's head. "You're so clever!"

"But what are we thinking?" said Miss Sweetbeak. "Cleaning Friendship Forest and saving Christmas is more important than wedding dresses."

Holly grinned. "I've an idea how to get everything clean, all at once! Follow me!"

Goldie picked up the basket of Toasty Toffee jars, and they all hurried after Holly. They took care not to slip on the sludgy paths as they headed towards Willowtree River.

When they reached it, Holly opened

her bottle. "I'll tip these into the water," she said. "It should make enough Bubble Flower Paint Power to clean the whole forest. Including the Unique Boutique!"

She poured most of the crystals into the river. Almost at once a big blue bubble bobbed up to the surface – *blub!* It drifted on to the riverbank. Then another bobbed up … and another …

The first bubble landed and burst on a

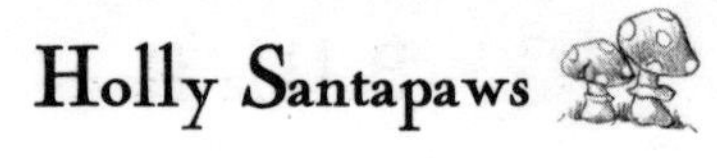

mud-spattered clump of feather grass.

Pop!

The grass was suddenly spotless and shining pink again.

Pop! went the next bubble … and the next …

As they popped, the dirt disappeared.

Blub! Blub! Blub!

Pop! Pop! Pop!

Miss Sweetbeak and the four friends were soon surrounded by big blubbing bubbles.

"It's like being up in the blue sky!" Jess laughed delightedly.

"Or down in the sea!" said Lily.

As the bubbles began to clear, they stared in astonishment.

"Everything's spotless!" said Jess. "What a brilliant invention!"

Holly's tail wagged. "It wasn't invented to clean things, it was supposed to paint things," she said, "but it's pretty useful! I think I'll give some to my cousins, the Swiftpaw husky dogs. They get so muddy on sledging trips."

"At this rate, the whole forest will soon be clean," Miss Sweetbeak said happily. "Christmas will be saved!"

"The bubbles should have cleaned everything in your boutique, too," said Goldie. "Now we need to plug up the Confetti Shower."

As they watched the bubbles float through the trees, they heard a cross voice.

Grizelda's sleigh was weaving through the treetops.

The friends ducked behind a lemon berry bush and watched it land.

Lily held Holly close and whispered, "Oh no! What will Grizelda do when she sees what we've done?"

CHAPTER FIVE

Confetti Shower Chaos

The girls heard Grizelda grumbling at her ice creatures.

"Why do you need a drink?" she snapped. "You're made of ice!"

The creatures pulled at their harness and dipped their heads into the river. They gulped water so greedily that Jess

and Lily felt sorry for them.

"Grizelda must work them very hard," Jess said quietly.

"While they're drinking," Lily whispered, "let's go and plug up the Confetti Shower."

The girls took handfuls of Toasty Toffees from Holly's jars and moulded them into one big sticky ball.

While Grizelda stood on the riverbank, nagging her thirsty ice creatures, Jess crept over to the Confetti Shower and jammed the sticky sweets into its nozzle. Then she scurried back to the others.

Grizelda returned to the sleigh, muttering, "Those interfering girls have managed to clean the forest, but I'll soon muck it up again!"

The watching friends giggled as she picked up the Confetti Shower.

Grizelda spun around. "Huh? Who's that?"

"Yip!" Holly yelped. "She heard us!"

The witch strode around the lemon berry bush.

"You!" she shrieked. "The silly girls and the nosy cat, meddling again! And you've got new friends, have you?" She peered at Miss Sweetbeak and Holly, who cowered behind Jess.

"A snowy owl and a white puppy with grubby feet, eh?" snarled Grizelda. "Well, you'll soon be grubby all over!"

She pointed the Confetti Shower at the friends and pressed the start button.

Holly closed her eyes tight, but instead of spitting out dirt, the machine sputtered.

"It won't work!" Lily cried. "It's bunged up!"

"Pah!" Grizelda snapped, and tried again.

BANG!

The Confetti Shower exploded. The back of the machine popped and mud squirted all over Grizelda. She screamed in fury. Her clothes and green hair dripped with muck.

Gobbets of mud dropped from her chin as she flung the Confetti Shower aside and climbed into her sleigh.

"Useless machine!" she shrieked. "Nasty girls! I'll get you! My plan's only just begun!"

She shook the reins and the sleigh lurched away, pulled by her ice creatures.

Lily hugged Jess joyfully. "Holly's sweet invention spoiled Grizelda's plan!" she said. "Hooray!"

Miss Sweetbeak kissed the excited puppy. "You've stopped Christmas from being ruined, Holly! Good job!"

Holly smiled happily. "Thanks! Too bad Mr. Cleverfeather's invention is broken, though."

Jess collected the Confetti Shower. "Let's take it to him," she said. "He'll fix it."

They tramped through clean snow, heading for the elderly owl's tree. As they followed a path edged with tall pine trees, Holly found something lying on the snow.

"Yip! It's a paper kite!" she said.

Lily examined it. "It's been made from

a page in Mr Cleverfeather's invention book," she said. "See? It's covered in notes and diagrams." She turned the paper over. "Oh no!"

"What?" asked Jess.

Lily showed her.

"*MELP HE!*"

The friends were horrified.

"Mr Cleverfeather needs help!" said Jess.

Miss Sweetbeak's eyes filled with tears. "Please," she said. "We must save him!"

The girls put their arms around her. "We will," said Lily.

Jess nodded. "Somehow."

Story Two
Magic Bells

CHAPTER ONE

Poor Mr Cleverfeather

Goldie, Miss Sweetbeak, Holly and the girls stood beneath the pine trees, wondering what to do. Lily clutched Mr Cleverfeather's desperate plea for help, written on a paper kite.

Miss Sweetbeak was so upset that Jess and Lily told her to fly home and make sure the mess Grizelda had created in her boutique had been cleaned by Holly's Bubble Flower Paint Power.

"We'll find out why Mr Cleverfeather needs help," said Lily. "Grizelda's behind it, I'm sure."

"And we won't let her spoil Christmas, or your wedding," Jess promised.

As Miss Sweetbeak flew off, the friends hurried to Mr Cleverfeather's tree. When they reached it, they were dismayed to see Grizelda's sleigh nearby, with the ice creatures biting the blades of grass poking through the snow.

Goldie pointed to the top of Mr Cleverfeather's spiral staircase. The witch was backing out of his shed, dragging a large green box with levers and buttons on top.

Holly gasped. "Grizelda! She's in Mr Cleverfeather's shed!"

"And she's got the Merry Melody Machine!" Jess cried.

"You might have stopped my dirty

plan," sneered Grizelda, "but the silly owl has lots more inventions I can use." She cackled with laughter. "Now I've captured him, I'll make him show me how to use them. I'll ruin Christmas and I'll ruin the forest for good. Soon the animals will leave, and it will be mine. All mine!"

She touched a bony finger to the doorknob, chanting:

"Trapped inside with a magical lock,
Don't try to call or ring or knock.
As I possess the magical key.
Friendship Forest will belong to me!"

Grizelda snapped her fingers. The ice creatures leapt into the air and hovered beside the shed, while she heaved the green box onto the sleigh.

"Yah!" The witch shook the reins and cackled as Christmas carols began to play from Mr Cleverfeather's machine. The ice creatures pulled away across the treetops.

As the sleigh flew off, a sad figure with drooping shoulders appeared at the shed window.

"Mr Cleverfeather!" Lily called. She cupped her hands around her mouth. "Are you OK?"

He gave a slow, sad nod.

"Cheer up!" said Jess. "We're going to rescue you!"

The owl shook his head. "Make sure the forest is safe from Grizelda first!" he shouted. "Hollow fer!"

Goldie looked puzzled.

"He means 'Follow her!'" Lily explained.

"He's right," said Jess. "We must do

whatever it takes to save the forest."

"And Christmas," said Holly.

Jess shouted to Mr Cleverfeather, "We'll be back as soon as possible!"

"Come on, everyone," said Lily. "After that witch!"

They ran through the trees, desperately trying to keep the sleigh in sight. They raced across a meadow where frosted silver snowflakes hovered magically in mid-air, then passed a copse of Christmas trees, covered with red and gold ribbon bows and topped with glistening stars. The decorations looked lovely – but they couldn't enjoy them.

Holly stopped in a hollow with tall rocks on either side. "I can't see Grizelda's sleigh!" she said anxiously.

Lily jumped on to a rock to scan the sky. "Shh, everyone," she said. "Listen for the music."

The sound of a flute playing

"Ding Dong Merrily On High" floated through the air.

Suddenly Holly gave a yip. "There's the sleigh!" she cried, pointing to three tall hills with rounded tops, covered with a thick blanket of snow. Lily thought they looked just like iced buns.

The puppy scratched her head. "Those are the Heathertop Hills," she said. "What's Grizelda up to?"

"I don't know," said Goldie, "but I have a bad feeling about this ..."

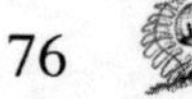

CHAPTER TWO

Avalanche!

Mr Cleverfeather's music suddenly changed. Instead of bells, flutes and a tinkling piano, there was the scratchy sound of a screechy violin, a honking trumpet and clattery drums.

The friends covered their ears.

"That's terrible!" said Lily, as the shriek

of a flute being blown too hard joined the other instruments.

"It's witchy music!" Goldie shouted.

Holly yelped. "It hurts my ears!"

Jess scooped her up, snuggled her into her coat and pulled the puppy's red hat over her fluffy ears.

The music grew so loud

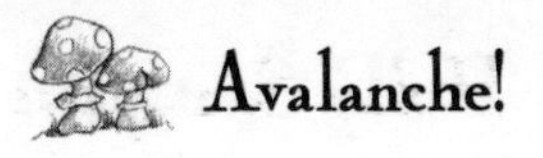

they felt the ground rumble.

Lily jumped. “It’s like an earthquake!”

The horrible screeching blasted through the forest and Goldie pointed to the hilltops. “Look!”

Giant snowballs were rolling down the Heathertop Hills, slowly at first, then faster and faster. They gathered more snow as they rolled downhill.

“They’re growing!” Lily shouted.

The giant snowballs grew even larger as they thundered down towards the forest.

“Avalanche!” Goldie

cried in horror. "RUN!"

The girls sprinted after her.

"This way!" Goldie darted to a tall rock with an overhanging ledge. They huddled beneath it as several huge snowballs thundered overhead and hit the ground in an explosion of powdery snow.

The music carried on blaring.

"Is everyone OK?" Goldie shouted.

"Yes," the others replied shakily.

"But what about the forest?" asked Holly.

Great heaps of snow had smothered plants and bushes everywhere, smashing

down flowers and branches.

Jess looked up to see the ice creatures galloping through the air, with the sleigh swooping behind them. The music blasted louder still, and now Grizelda screeched along with it.

"Smother the horrible Friendship Forest.

Bury it deep in mountains of snow.

I want it just for me, me, me.

Those nasty animals have to GO!"

Holly burst into tears. "She is just wicked!"

Once the witch had passed, they ventured out. Thick snow lay everywhere

and, on the hills, more avalanches had been triggered by the loud music.

Little animals scurried up on to rooftops or climbed trees to escape the danger.

"We have to do something," Lily said. "The animals' homes will get swallowed up by snow."

"She's burying Christmas!" Holly whimpered.

"You're right," said Jess. "I can't see a

single twinkling light."

Holly's whiskers drooped. Her ears and her tail drooped, too. "Suppose she dumps more and more snow? Suppose she covers the whole forest?"

Lily hugged the puppy tightly. "We won't let her," she said firmly. "We will stop Grizelda. What's more, we'll do it in time for Christmas."

"And the wedding," said Goldie.

"We need to get Grizelda away from the Merry Melody Machine before she causes any more avalanches," said Jess. "Then we'll rescue Mr Cleverfeather."

"And find a way to melt the snow," said Goldie.

It was a lot to do, in not very much time.

Lily had an idea. "Holly, you said your dancing shoes went wrong, didn't you? That they won't stop dancing?"

The puppy nodded sadly.

"Then," Lily said with a grin, "I've an idea that might just work!"

CHAPTER THREE

Silver Boots

"Let's trick Grizelda into putting on those shoes Holly invented!" said Lily. "She'll be dancing all over the place – she'd never be able to catch us!"

Holly stared. "You mean my dancing shoes can be used after all?"

Goldie sighed. "It's a good idea but

there isn't time to go all the way back to your workshop."

Holly clasped Goldie's paws. "Billy Stoutfoot the goat will give me some shoes. I can fix them just like the other pair!"

"Billy Stoutfoot?" asked Jess. They hadn't met this animal before.

"He's the forest cobbler," Goldie explained. "He makes and mends shoes."

Holly bounced excitedly. "Let's go!"

Lily picked her up. "Little puppies can't trudge through deep snow," she said. "You tell us the way."

After a slippery walk along an icy pathway, Holly showed them a corn-coloured door set in the foot of a hillside. It was almost hidden by heaped snow.

Jess tapped on the door with its shoe-shaped knocker, and out came Billy

Stoutfoot. He was a golden-brown goat with curved horns, and he wore shiny green boots.

"Welcome!"

he said. "But what are you doing out in this terrible snow?"

Lily explained what was happening. "We wondered," she finished, "if you have a pair of witch-sized shoes. We want to distract Grizelda while we get hold of the Merry Melody Machine."

"Baa! So that witch was behind the avalanches," Billy said. "Well, I've just the thing. I've been making a large pair of silver boots to hang outside, so everyone can see where to come for excellent footwear."

He went to his workbench to fetch them.

"They're perfect!" said Jess.

Billy brought out a round box with buttons stuck all over the lid. "Look in my accessories box for something to decorate the boots." He laughed. "Baa-ha-ha! I haven't anything shaped like warty toads or cauldrons, but you'll find something."

While Goldie and the girls burrowed through the accessories, Holly asked if she could borrow Billy's cobbling tools. "I need to alter the boots," she explained.

The accessories box was full of fabric flowers, painted china buttons, shiny buckles and silky tassels.

"There's nothing witchy," Lily said, disappointed.

But Jess spotted something gleaming at the bottom of the box. She pulled out some glittering purple gems the size of acorns.

"Grizelda will love these!" said Goldie. "She's always greedy for jewels."

They took them to the workbench where Holly's puppy paws seemed to fly over the silver boots. She finished by fixing a little red bell to the back of each.

"Magic bells!" she said.

The girls stuck the purple gems on the

toes with Billy's strong glue.

"Done!" said Lily.

"Thanks to Holly and Billy," Jess added.

They said goodbye to the cheery cobbler and set off in search of Grizelda.

The music blasting through the forest

grew louder, and soon Goldie's sharp eyes spotted the witch's icy sleigh flying towards Mr Cleverfeather's tree.

"She's probably going to steal more inventions," said Holly.

They ran after the sleigh, and were just in time to see it land. The witch was about to climb the tree when she noticed Holly's Wonders Workshop.

"What have we here?" she said, going to investigate.

"Quick!" said Lily. "Leave the boots where she'll see them."

Jess dashed to a tree stump and stood

the boots on it. As the screechy music blared, the friends darted behind a bush, covering their ears.

Grizelda peered through Holly's window. "Pah!" she said. "Call those inventions? Load of junk!"

Holly jumped up crossly. "Horrid witch!"

"Ssh!" Lily pulled her down. "She'll soon learn what a good inventor you are!"

Grizelda turned and spotted the silver boots. "Ooh!" She looked closer. "Ooh!" She kicked off her pointy black boots to

reveal purple and green striped stockings. "These boots are wet," she said. "I'll take the new ones!"

She slipped her knobbly feet into them.

Instantly, the little magic bells began to jangle. Grizelda's feet jerked and kicked. The bells jangled even more.

"She's dancing!" giggled Jess.

"Whoa!" shrieked Grizelda, as she twirled and skipped between the trees. "Whoa! I can't stop! He-elp!"

Suddenly, Jess charged towards the witch.

Lily leapt up. "Stop!" she cried. "Jess, what are you doing? Come back!"

CHAPTER FOUR

The Merry Melody Machine

As the whirling witch danced a high-stepping jig, Lily watched Jess rush forward and snatch something from her cloak pocket. Grizelda was shrieking and spinning so fast that she didn't notice.

Jess ran back to the others. "Look!" She

held up a golden key.

Lily gasped. "Grizelda's magic key!" she yelled over the deafening music.

Jess hugged Holly. "I couldn't have got it without your invention!" she shouted.

Holly beamed with pride.

Grizelda danced away, squealing angrily.

Goldie looked anxious. "Let's get the

Merry Melody Machine from the sleigh before Grizelda's ice creatures drag it off."

"Wait till they're looking the other way," said Jess.

The ice creatures began biting at grass tips.

"This is our chance to sneak up on them," said Goldie.

Jess and Lily crept to the sleigh, grabbed the music machine and carried it back to the others. The noise was horrible.

"Holly," Lily shouted, "do you think you can stop the music before it causes another avalanche?"

Holly examined the levers and buttons, then shook her head. "It's Mr Cleverfeather's newest invention," she said. "I don't know how it works." Her whiskers drooped. "If only I had his notebook."

Jess had a sudden, hopeful thought. "Hey, wasn't Mr Cleverfeather's kite made from a page of his notebook?" She pulled it out of her pocket and looked at the words underneath his scrawled message. "Yes!"

She showed the others. The page he'd written on had the design for the Merry

Melody Machine on it.

"Mr Cleverfeather must have seen Grizelda coming and guessed what she was after," said Goldie. "That's why he used this sheet. It was to help us stop her!"

She passed it to Holly, who pored over the paper, muttering to herself. Without another word she fetched a spanner and screwdriver from her workshop and started

tinkering with the screeching machine. The puppy's paws flitted over the buttons and levers and, suddenly, the terrible music stopped.

Goldie and the girls swooped down to hug her. "You did it!" they cried. "Hooray for Holly!"

The little puppy's tail wagged so fast it was a blur.

Lily grinned. "Now let's rescue Mr Cleverfeather."

Jess waved the magic key. "It'll be easy with this!"

Holly laughed. "Especially as Grizelda's

busy dancing!" She pointed through to where the witch was still high-kicking and shrieking and twirling round trees.

Goldie searched the sky. "And no ice creatures in sight!"

They hurried through the snow, with the girls carrying the Merry Melody Machine between them. But as they drew near to Mr Cleverfeather's tree, they found Miss Sweetbeak in a terrible flap.

"Oh, my dears, I'm sad to glee you," she said. "No – glad to see you! I flew over to make sure Mr Cleverfeather was all right after those dreadful avalanches,

and … well, just look!"

She pointed upwards with a white wingtip.

The friends gasped. Mr Cleverfeather's inventing shed was almost completely smothered by snow. They could only see the roof and chimney.

"A huge snowball must have hit the tree!" said Jess.

"How can we get him out?" cried Lily.

Miss Sweetbeak flapped her wings anxiously. "There's only one thing to do," she said. "Quickly, my dears. To the Winter Wonders!"

CHAPTER FIVE

Rescue!

The sun was low as Lily, Jess, Goldie and Holly stood before three pedestals that held the Winter Wonders: the sugarplum, the snowflake and the snowdrop.

Miss Sweetbeak went to the snowdrop, spread her white wings and said,

"You bring snow to Friendship Forest,

Whenever
your petals
are twinkling.
Take away this
deep, cold snow,
And leave just a lovely
sprinkling."

The silver tips of the snowdrop's petals twinkled, and the snow all around began to disappear. Soon only a crisp, frosty dusting was left, sparkling in the last of the wintry sunlight.

"How did you do that?" asked Lily.

Miss Sweetbeak smiled. "I know a thing or two about snow," she said. "I am a snowy owl, after all!"

"Let's hurry to Mr Cleverfeather's tree!" cried Goldie. "It'll soon be dark, and he'll be cold."

With the deep snow gone, the journey was much quicker this time. When they got to the tree, they were relieved to see that the snowdrift had vanished and they could see the inventing shed. While Miss Sweetbeak fluttered up to the shed, Lily touched the tree trunk to make the staircase appear, and they all climbed up.

Jess touched the doorknob with the magic key. The door sprang open and Mr Cleverfeather came out. When he saw Miss Sweetbeak, he threw his wings around her.

"I've been worried about you, my love." He planted a kiss on Miss Sweetbeak's forehead.

She giggled and pecked him back. "I'm so glad you're safe. Now I must go and shake more – I mean make sure – everything's ready for the wedding," she said. "Bye!" She flew off.

When the girls told Mr Cleverfeather that they'd defeated Grizelda, with lots of help from Holly, he looked very proud indeed.

"What a part smuppy," he said. "I mean, smart puppy!" Then he added anxiously, "The Sparklehoof reindeer are still missing, so we've no wedding sleigh. And do you remember my Ice Device that went missing? I invented it to make ice sculptures for our wedding feast. Grizelda kept asking me how it works. Of course I didn't tell her, but what if she works it out?"

"Do you think she's got it?" asked Goldie.

Mr Cleverfeather nodded. "I think she's planning something horrible – her grand finale for Christmas Day!"

Jess and Lily shared a worried glance.

Goldie settled Mr Cleverfeather in his armchair and wrapped a blanket around his shoulders. "It's late," she said.

"We'll never find the Ice Device or the Sparklehoofs in the dark. We must all rest if we're to stop Grizelda tomorrow."

"I am a sit bleepy – I mean – a bit sleepy!" yawned Mr Cleverfeather. His eyes drooped closed and within moments he was snoring with a soft 'twit-twoo'.

"Let's leave him in peace," whispered Goldie as they tiptoed out.

"Ooh, let's have a sleepover at my den!" said Holly.

The girls knew that no time passed in their world while they were in Friendship Forest, so they agreed at once. They were determined to make sure Grizelda didn't spoil the wedding – or Christmas.

As they walked to Holly's home, their way was lit by hundreds of twinkling Christmas lights. Soon, the puppy stopped by a sky-blue door tucked among thick tree roots.

She sniffed. "Mmm, Mum's baking! Come in!"

Paper chains, scarlet holly berries and glow-worm lanterns decorated the den. A sparkling Christmas tree stood in the corner, dotted with baubles and draped with silver tinsel.

Mrs Santapaws wore a pink-and-white checked apron, and had flour on her nose. She welcomed the friends, then handed around freshly baked ginger cookies and strawberry tarts.

"I've been baking all day," she said. "It's Christmas tomorrow and Holly's cousins, the Swiftpaw husky dogs, are coming to celebrate with us."

Everyone ate till they were full, then they finished off a huge pot of hot chocolate. Holly fell asleep on Lily's lap, and soon Goldie and the girls felt sleepy, too. Mrs Santapaws fetched cosy blankets for them, and they snuggled into big squishy armchairs by the crackling log fire.

"It's going to be a very merry Christmas," Jess smiled. "As long as Grizelda stays away."

Story Three
Wedding Bells

CHAPTER ONE

Breakfast with the Santapawses

Jess, Lily, Holly and Goldie woke to jingling bells and shouts of "Merry Christmas!"

They jumped up and flung open the curtains.

A great sledge pulled by four silvery

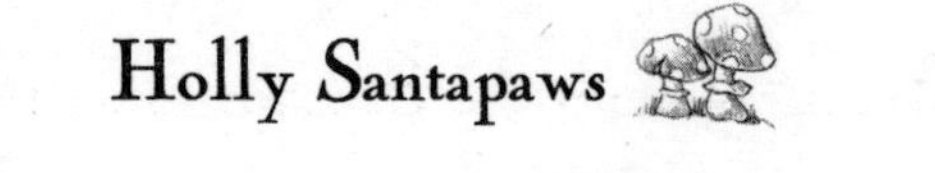

husky dogs stood outside. It was piled with presents. Sitting on top were three adorable, wriggly puppies.

"It's my cousins, the Swiftpaws," cried Holly as she ran outside to greet them.

Jess and Lily gave Goldie Merry Christmas hugs, thinking how funny it was to have an extra Christmas Day

this year! But they hadn't forgotten that today they had to stop Grizelda ruining both Christmas and Mr Cleverfeather's wedding.

Just then, Holly and her parents burst into the sitting room. The whole Swiftpaw family followed, leaving muddy footprints everywhere.

Holly giggled. "Look at your dirty feet, Swiftpaws! I've got an invention just for you!"

Jess and Lily laughed. They knew that the Bubble Flower Paint Power would soon do the job!

When everyone and everything was clean, all the puppies jumped over to everyone for lots of Christmas hugs. The Swiftpaws were delighted to meet the girls.

"We've heard how you stand up to Grizelda," said Granny Swiftpaw. She introduced them to Mr and Mrs Swiftpaw and their three puppies, Zippy, Mush and little Anji.

"You're brave!" said Anji. "I'll be brave like you when I grow up, and I'll be clever like Holly too!"

"Here's your Christmas present, Holly,"

said Zippy, handing her a parcel.

The excited puppy opened it. It was a brand-new tool kit. She held it high so everyone could see. "Thanks, everyone!" But then she frowned, as if she was thinking. "Hang on a minute!" she said, and ran off, leaving Mrs Swiftpaw looking a bit confused. A few minutes later Holly returned with sticky paws and an empty Toasty Toffee jar. "I fixed the brake on your sledge. Remember, you told me it was a bit loose."

"Oh yes!" Mrs Swiftpaw said. "Thank you, Holly."

The girls helped Mr Santapaws make breakfast. There were pancakes with berry sauce, toasted buns with "Ho ho ho" iced on them, and cinnamon porridge with honey drizzled over it.

When everyone was full, Mrs Santapaws announced, "Time for the rest of the presents!"

As the puppies bounced excitedly, Jess said, "We'd love to stay, but we have to find out what Grizelda's planning to do with the Ice Device. We can't let her ruin Christmas." She noticed the Swiftpaw puppies' horrified faces. "We won't let her ruin it," she promised.

"We must find the Sparklehoofs, too," said Goldie.

"And save Mr Cleverfeather's wedding," added Jess.

Holly jumped up. "I'm coming too! You'll need me to fix things!"

"Of course we will," said Lily. "We can't

do it without you!"

They said goodbye and went outside, where a sprinkling of snow lay like a glistening carpet. It was chilly, but the sun was shining, and the forest looked beautiful. They walked beneath trees decorated with glittering baubles. Fine silver tinsel was draped across their branches, like gossamer webs. Everywhere looked Christmassy.

Soon the friends reached a group of spectacular flowers and bushes made of ice, sparkling in the sunlight.

Lily clapped her hands. "Ice sculptures!

Mr Cleverfeather must have found his Ice Device. They're lovely!"

As the friends drew near to Miss Sweetbeak's Unique Boutique, they spotted a sculpture of a flying swan that had been created in mid-air.

"It's beautiful," cried Holly, "and it looks so real!"

"And see the ice butterflies?" said Goldie. "They're just like Flitta and Popsy, our butterfly friends!"

She knocked on Miss Sweetbeak's door. There was no answer, so Goldie opened it and they all went inside, calling,

"Merry Christmas!"

Their smiles faded. The girls stared in shock at a figure standing in the room. It was Miss Sweetbeak in her wedding dress. But she was completely encased in ice.

Goldie gasped. "She's been frozen solid!"

CHAPTER TWO

An Icy Problem

Jess's face was pale. "Miss Sweetbeak has been turned into an ice sculpture!"

"The flying swan!" cried Goldie. "The butterflies! Those weren't ice sculptures, they were real creatures!"

Lily scooped Holly into her arms and cuddled her. "This means Grizelda's got the Ice Device," she said. "She must have put a spell on it. Instead of creating animal sculptures, it's turning all the animals into sculptures!"

Holly's eyes filled with tears.

Jess dropped a kiss on the puppy's fluffy head. "Don't worry," she said. "We'll find Grizelda and get the device back. We'll reverse it somehow, and find a way to unfreeze Miss Sweetbeak."

But it all had to be done in time for the wedding. And there wasn't long to go!

They set off through the forest, following an icy trail. Soon they saw two hares, frozen with their ears flattened back in fright. Birds stood icily stiff on branches, and Woody Flufftail the squirrel had been frozen in mid-air as he leapt between two trees.

Holly hid her face in her paws. "This is

horrible!" she whimpered.

"We'll make it all right," Lily whispered, desperately hoping they could.

"It looks like Grizelda was heading for her tower," said Goldie. "Let's find a boat to take us across Shimmer Lake."

But when they reached Shimmer Lake, they stared in dismay. It was just a wide sheet of ice. The witch had frozen it.

Goldie examined the icy surface. "It's very thin. It would crack under our weight."

Jess frowned. "It will take too long to go around the lake. Grizelda will have

carried out her plan before we get there." She sighed. "I wish we could cross that ice safely."

Holly's ears perked up. "The Swiftpaws' sledge! They move so fast the ice wouldn't have a chance to crack beneath it!"

"Wonderful!" said Goldie. "I'll send a butterfly message!" She put her paws together, then flapped them like wings.

A purple butterfly flew down on

to her shoulder. Her antennae were drooping.

"My name is Hermia. My friends have been frozen!" the butterfly said in her tinkly voice. "Who would do that?"

"Grizelda!" said Lily, Jess and Holly together.

"Don't worry," said Jess. "We'll unfreeze your friends. But first, will you take a message to the Swiftpaw family at Holly's den?"

Hermia's antennae lifted a little. "I'll flutter faster than the breeze!"

CHAPTER THREE

Grizelda's Tower

Not long after Hermia had flown off, the friends heard a pounding noise as something charged through the forest.

"What's that?" Jess asked, alarmed. "Is it Grizelda's sleigh?"

Goldie's ears twitched. "I don't think so," she said. "It's got bells on!"

They huddled behind a tree, then smiled in relief as the four grown-up Swiftpaws burst through the trees, pulling their sledge. The Christmas bells on either side of the sledge were jingling merrily and the dogs yapped their hellos.

"Thanks for coming," Lily said to Grandpa Swiftpaw.

"Glad to help," he replied. "The puppies stayed in the Santapaws family's den, so there's plenty of room. Hop aboard!"

"Not you, Holly," said Mrs Swiftpaw. "There's a special place for you at the front with Grandma. You can lead us!"

Holly was thrilled! Grandpa helped her into her harness, and off they sped, across the frozen lake. The ice creaked as they glided across it.

"Faster!" cried Goldie. "If we slow down, the ice will crack!"

Everyone was relieved to reach the far bank and the shelter of the woods beside Grizelda's dismal grey tower.

"It looks scary," whispered Holly, as she undid her harness. "Even the door knocker's got a scary monster face."

"It's cobwebby and mouldy inside," said Goldie.

"And dark and gloomy," said Lily.

"Smelly, too," added Jess.

Goldie pointed to the top of the tower where there was a terrace with a low wall around the edge.

Grizelda's sleigh was parked there.

Beside it was a blue-and-white contraption, with spikes like icicles sticking out all over.

"It must be the Ice Device!" Goldie said excitedly. "We need to get up there!"

"How?" asked Lily. "We're not expert climbers like you."

"I wish we could fly, like Grizelda's sleigh," said Jess.

"Or climb like squirrels," said Lily.

Holly gave a little bounce. "You can!" she said, and scampered back to the sledge. She returned waving a jar of Toasty Toffees and a handful of tools.

"I left these on the sledge when I mended it. Put Toasty Toffees on the bottom of your boots. They'll stick to the wall as you climb!"

"What a clever idea!" said Jess.

Holly stuck clumps of Toasty Toffees to the girls' boot soles. They took some for their hands, too.

"Holly, we'll need you to fix the Ice Device," said Jess. "I'll carry you inside my coat."

"And I'll put your tools in my pockets," said Lily.

The girls followed Goldie, climbing up

the tower. It was easy when their fingertips and feet stuck to the rough stone.

At last they tumbled over the low wall on to the terrace.

Lily hugged Holly. "Your idea worked brilliantly!" she said.

"Shh!" said Jess. "Be quiet, or

Grizelda might hear us."

"What's that?" Holly asked, pointing to a tree in a tub. Its thorns were like long needles. Dangling from its branches were cut-outs of black bats, with glowing red eyes. On top was a scruffy crow with a beak cut from a liquorice plant, and around the pot was a ring of rats made out of old black tights that didn't look very clean.

"It's Grizelda's Christmas tree!" said Goldie. "Ugh!"

"She could be back any minute," said Lily. "Let's hurry. Holly, you try to reverse the Ice Device, and we'll keep guard." She gave the puppy her tools.

The friends spread out, keeping watch while Holly worked. She banged, tugged and loosened the different parts of the machine. It looked like very complicated work.

Goldie pointed to the sky. "The ice creatures are coming!"

"Hurry, Holly!" cried Lily.

"Almost there," said Holly.

But she needed a little extra time.

"I know!" said Jess. "Snowballs!"

She gathered snow into her hands and flung a snowball at the ice creatures. Lily and Goldie did the same. The snowballs hit the ice creatures but they kept flying straight. The ice creatures landed with a clatter of hooves. A flurry of snowballs didn't bother them.

Holly pulled the Ice Device out of the way, but it slipped and fell on its side. There was a loud click as the icicle spikes started spraying.

"Look out!" cried Lily. "It's shooting ice everywhere!"

But it wasn't ice. It was a silvery mist. And warm!

"You've done it, Holly!" cried Goldie.

The device sprayed all over the ice

creatures. With a ripple and a shimmer, they began to change. The ice was melting!

A moment later, the friends gasped. Before them stood three animals with soft brown fur and velvety antlers.

"Reindeer!" cried Lily.

Goldie clapped her paws. "Not just any reindeer," she said joyfully. "Meet the Sparklehoof family!"

CHAPTER FOUR

Berry, Ivy and Mistletoe

The girls couldn't believe that Grizelda's ice creatures had been the Sparklehoofs all along!

"Thank you for freeing us," said the biggest reindeer. "I'm Mistletoe, and my sisters are Berry and Ivy. We were on

our way to Mr Cleverfeather's yesterday, when Grizelda appeared and aimed that machine at us."

"She chanted a spell and turned us to ice," said Berry.

"We're so glad to be free," said Ivy, "but we should leave before Grizelda—"

Clomping footsteps stomped up the spiral stairway.

"Grizelda!" cried Lily. "We've got to go."

"Climb on to the sleigh!" cried Mistletoe.

The witch appeared at the end of

the terrace. She turned purple with fury and her green hair whipped around her face like angry snakes.

"You horrible, meddling girls!" she screamed. "You rotten animals! You think you'll ruin my plan? Pah!"

As the friends scrambled on to the sleigh, Grizelda lunged forward and snatched at Holly's paw.

The little puppy dodged the bony hand, raced across the terrace and jumped on to the low wall.

Lily grabbed the Sparklehoofs' reins and steered the sleigh between Grizelda and Holly.

Jess leaned over, scooping Holly into her arms, and the Sparklehoofs leapt into the air.

Grizelda shrieked in fury and shook her fists as the friends flew away.

They hugged one another and waved to the Swiftpaws, who were already on

the other side of the lake, racing back to Holly's home.

"Let's unfreeze the lake," said Goldie.

Holly grinned and held the Ice Device above the frozen lake. As the warm mist sprayed over it, the ice melted. Fish leapt into the air and splashed back into the water.

As they flew over the forest, Lily looked down and smiled. "Everything looks so

Christmassy!"

The dusting of snow on the trees and ground sparkled in the wintry sunlight. Here and there, animals wrapped in warm scarves greeted one another and exchanged gifts.

The sleigh flew lower, heading for Miss Sweetbeak's boutique. As they passed the frozen animals, Holly pointed the Ice Device at them and freed them.

"Thanks, Holly!" cried the

Longwhiskers rabbits, who'd been frozen as they served Christmas cake at the Toadstool Café.

The swan stretched her great wings, crying, "What a relief!"

More cries of "Thanks!" and "Merry Christmas!" echoed through the forest. A Christmas choir of birds singing "The Holly and the Ivy" drifted up to the sleigh.

"Merry Christmas, everyone!"

called the friends.

When they landed beside the Unique Boutique, Jess and Lily carried the Ice Device inside and watched Holly unfreeze Miss Sweetbeak.

As the ice melted, the girls stared in delight. The snowy owl looked even lovelier than she had before. Her wedding dress was snow-white lace, dotted with sparkling silver sequins. She wore a dainty tiara, topped with strands of pearls that fluttered as she moved.

"Miss Sweetbeak, you look wonderful!" Lily said. "Are you OK?"

"Yes," said Miss Sweetbeak, "but I had such a shock! I was looking in my mirror when that horrid Grizelda appeared behind me. As I turned around, I was frozen!" She hugged the girls. "How can I ever thank you all for rescuing me?"

Jess laughed. "By getting married, of course!"

Holly bounced up and down. "Hooray! Wedding time!"

The wedding was held in Silver Glade, where frosted silver birch branches formed an arch over the aisle. The nearby

Treasure Tree was decorated with silver bells and sparkling candles. It was always laden with food the animals needed, but today there were crystallised fruits and candy canes!

The animals wriggled excitedly on white chairs with scarlet cushions.

The Merry Melody Machine played softly as Jess and Lily walked hand-in-hand up the aisle in their feather-trimmed red dresses. They shared a smile. This was so exciting!

Goldie was waiting to perform the ceremony. Mr Cleverfeather stood with

her, wearing the beautiful embroidered waistcoat that Miss Sweetbeak had made him. His feathers gleamed.

When the watching animals said, "Aaaah!" the girls turned to see Holly trotting up the aisle, carrying a basket of red roses, and wearing a silver tiara.

The music changed to a gentle melody.

"I wrote this tune," Mr Cleverfeather whispered. "It's called 'The Owl's Serenade' and—"

He stared over the girls' shoulders.

Miss Sweetbeak stood at the end of the aisle. She raised her white wings, swept into the air and glided silently towards Mr Cleverfeather.

"You book lootiful," he whispered.

CHAPTER FIVE

A Christmas Wedding

Goldie held a lovely wedding ceremony. Wings, paws and hands clapped at the end, as Mr Cleverfeather and Mrs Sweetbeak shared a kiss.

As the couple walked back down the aisle, bells rang out from every branch of every tree in the glade.

Holly and the girls followed. At the end of the aisle, there were lots of hugs.

"Congratulations!" said Lily.

"Everyone to the Toadstool Café for the wedding feast!" said Mr Cleverfeather. "Gets low! I mean, let's go!"

The newlyweds climbed into the sleigh and set off. Everyone else followed, singing, "Happy wedding to you!"

Toadstool Glade was decorated with pink and silver "Just Married" banners made by Silvia Whitewing the swan. Agatha Glitterwing the magpie had

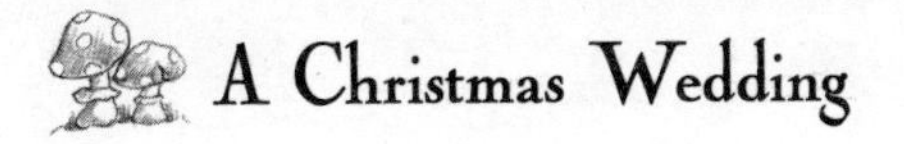

woven strings of tinkling bells through the trees. Robins wearing tiny red-and-white Christmas hats flew around sprinkling paper snowflakes over everyone.

The girls gazed at the Toadstool Café in delight. It had been transformed into a gingerbread house for Christmas! The tables were covered in white cloths embroidered with green holly and scarlet berries. Christmas crackers lay at each place, and three ice sculptures of reindeer stood in the middle.

Jess giggled. "I hope those aren't the Sparklehoofs!"

"They're not," laughed Ivy. "Thanks to you girls, Goldie and Holly."

When the guests pulled their crackers, paper hats unfolded and jumped onto their heads all by themselves. Tiny curling streamers shot into the air, and little toy penguins tumbled on to the table. They popped upright and waddled around.

The baby animals loved them!

The crackers held special gifts, too. Lily's was a carved wooden flower. "A lily!" she said.

Jess's was a carved wooden ball with a bell inside it. "My kitten, Pixie, will love this!" she said.

The Longwhiskers family brought out a huge tureen of sweetroot soup, golden potatoes roasted with hazelnut patties, tomato and walnut tarts, and a mushroom and chestnut pie. There were bowls of crisp strawberry meringues, all soft and chewy inside, iced raspberry

buns, and chocolate cream cake.

Jugs of smoothies, milkshakes and blackberry fizz stood on the tables, with warm honey milk for the reindeer.

When everyone was full, the Merry Music Machine played "The Owl Serenade". Mr Cleverfeather held out a wingtip to his bride.

She smiled. "I'd dove to lance. I mean—"

He smiled, too. "I woe not you mean!"

The girls couldn't believe how perfectly the elderly owl danced, sweeping his new wife gracefully around the floor.

Then Jess realised. "He's wearing the

shoes Holly made for him!"

The puppy grinned. "I made a last-minute tweak."

"You," said Lily, "are a very talented inventor!"

Jess nodded. "You saved the wedding, and you saved Christmas, too."

"We all saved Christmas!" Holly said proudly.

When the first dance was over, the

girls joined in with the Bunny Hop, the Squirrel Shake and the Hedgehog Hustle.

"Show us a new dance, Jess!" called Lola Velvetnose the mole.

"OK!" said Jess. "It's the Wiggle Jiggle Giggle!"

Lily stared. "What's that?"

Jess grinned. "I don't know. I'll make it up!"

Soon everyone was waving their arms in the air, wiggling and jiggling. The younger animals giggled so much they could hardly stand.

Mr and Mrs Cleverfeather had one

last dance, then it was time to leave for their honeymoon. As they said goodbye, the Confetti Shower sprinkled frosted snowflake confetti over them.

The happy owls flew to the sleigh.

"We're having our honeymoon on Snowcap Mountain," Mr Cleverfeather called. "Thanks, everyone, and bood guy!"

"But before we go," said Mrs Cleverfeather, "here's a special gift for

Goldie, and for Less, Hilly and Jolly!"

She threw down four silver roses.

"We'll be sack boon!" cried the bride, as the Sparklehoofs took off.

Jess and Lily were thrilled. "Thank you!" they called as the Cleverfeathers flew away.

Lily turned to Jess. "It's time for us to go, too."

Holly hugged them. "I'll miss you," she said.

Jess tickled her ears.

"We'll see you soon, I'm sure."

All their animal friends said goodbye, then Goldie, who was carrying a big bag, walked them to the Friendship Tree. Just before they reached it, Lily said, "We're still wearing our bridesmaids' dresses!"

"They're yours to keep," said Goldie. "They're Christmas presents!" She handed them the big bag. "Here are your own clothes."

"We'd better put them on," said Jess. "It would be hard to explain these dresses to our parents!"

When they were ready, Goldie hugged

them. "I'll come and fetch you soon," she promised, "especially if Grizelda causes trouble." She touched the tree and a door appeared.

Lily opened it, letting golden light spill out.

With a last wave, the girls stepped inside. Immediately they felt the tingle that meant they were returning to their proper size.

As the light faded they stepped back into Brightley Meadow, just in time to see a pair of geese taking off.

Jess giggled. "Maybe they're going on

honeymoon, too!"

Lily pulled a handful of snowflake confetti from her pocket and tossed it after the birds. Then the two friends joined hands and skipped back to Helping Paw Wildlife Hospital with silver roses in their pockets.

The End

Jess and Lily are off for an adventure on Magic Mountain! Can they stop wicked Grizelda from spoiling the magic?

Turn over for a sneak peek of the next adventure,

Pippa Hoppytail's Rocky Road

"Breakfast time!" called Lily Hart. Lily and her best friend, Jess Forester, were carrying buckets of feed out of the Helping Paw Wildlife Hospital.

Little guinea pig noses woffled at their fence and, in another run, three baby squirrels scampered around excitedly. They were ready for breakfast!

Jess and Lily set to work. Soon, nearly all the bowls were filled with carrots, nuts or fresh green leaves.

"Just the rabbits now," said Lily, crossing the lawn. "They were feeling much better yesterday, so I bet they'll want a big breakfast!"

The girls walked over to the rabbit run, but when they got there – it was empty!

Jess gasped. "Where are they?"

They looked in the hutches. There was nothing but straw.

Then Lily found a hole beneath the side of the run. "Oh no!" she cried. "The rabbits have escaped!"

"Quick! Search the garden!" said Jess.

They split up. Lily looked in the flowerbeds, and Jess checked Mrs Hart's vegetable patch. Lily spotted the tips of two ears behind a clump of daffodils, but when she reached it, the rabbit had vanished.

Jess saw a white tail bobbing behind a gooseberry bush. She crept over, but the bunny scampered away.

"If only the rabbits could talk, like they can in Friendship Forest," said Lily. "Then we could call after them, and try and find them."

Read

Pippa Hoppytail's Rocky Road

to find out what happens next!

Look out for the brand-new Magic Animal Friends series!

Series Six

www.magicanimalfriends.com